Los Amiguitos' FIESTA

(The Little Friends' FIESTA)

A SOUTHWESTERN STORYBOOK

Illustrated by Judith Donoho Shade

Story by Jean Thor Cook

Los Amiguitos' FIESTA

Text copyright   2001 Jean Thor Cook
Illustrations copyright   1994 Judith Donoho Shade

ISBN 0-9708940-0-7
Library of Congress Catalog Card Number 2001089065

The illustrations in this book were done in colored pencil

Edited by Lincoln Wilson

Printed in the United States of America
Starline Pinting
Albuquerque, New Mexico

Los Amiguitos' FIESTA

is dedicated to my blessed grandchildren-

Katie, Kara, Ben, Audrey, Tom, Nathaniel, Kristy, Annalise and Kastine-

who bring the spice of chili peppers,

the joy of Mexican fiestas,

and the warmth of sunny southwestern days

into the lives of all who know them.

Jean Thor Cook

Dedicated in loving memory to:

Joan "Dovie" Donoho, mother of the illustrator and

Judith Donoho Shade, illustrator

In a village where children live in pink houses and chili peppers hang by front doors, ten amiguitos (little friends) sat under a bright blue sky.

"Today we take our pets to the padre to be blessed," said Liliana (lee-lee-AHN-a). Liliana opened a large basket filled with many things to decorate the pets. The amiguitos (ah-mee-GUEE-tose) watched as Liliana brought out pots of paint, ribbons, flowers, bells and clothes.

Waddle, waddle, wiggle.

"Quack, quack, SQUAWK!"

Señor Carlos, Liliana's duck, plopped into the soft dirt beside her.

"Señor Carlos is loved by everyone in the village," said Gilberto (heel-BEAR-toe), patting the complaining duck.

"Quack, quack, SQUAWK!"

"Why is my duck so noisy?" Liliana asked the amiguitos, with a frown on her face. The children shook their heads. No one knew why Señor Carlos was squawking.

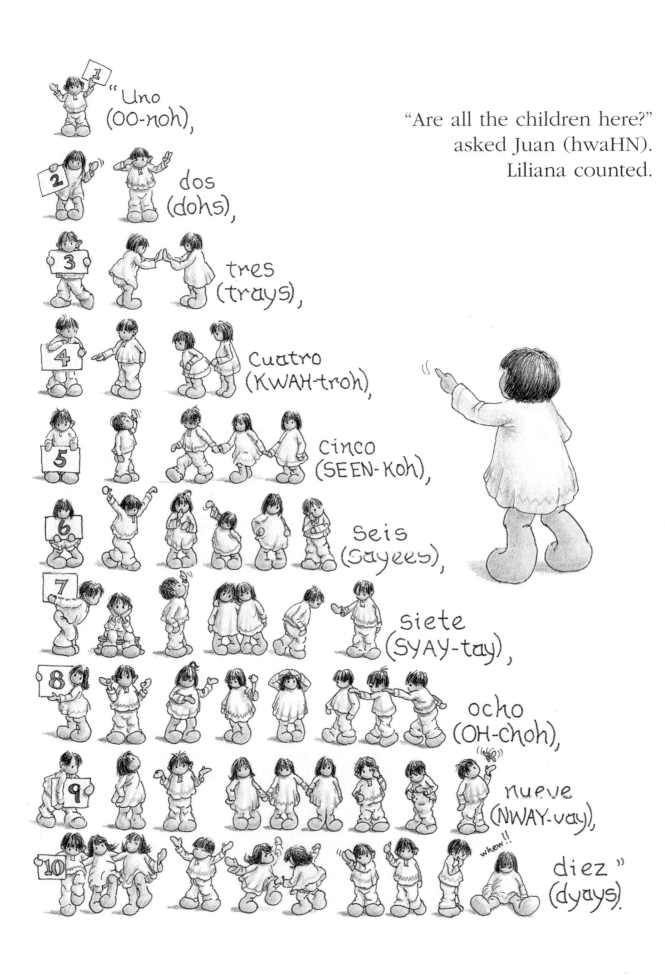

"Uno
(OO-noh),

dos
(dohs),

tres
(trays),

Cuatro
(KWAH-troh),

cinco
(SEEN-koh),

seis
(sayees),

siete
(SYAY-tay),

ocho
(OH-choh),

nueve
(NWAY-vay),

diez"
(dyays).

"Are all the children here?"
asked Juan (hwaHN).
Liliana counted.

whew!!

"Sí, there are ten, and everyone has their pets. Now we can begin," Liliana said, taking the decorations out of the basket.

"Quack, quack, SQUAWK!"

"You will be happy," Liliana told the grumbling duck, "when you parade in your new clothes to the blessing."

Liliana made a handsome vest for Señor Carlos.

She tied a sombrero on the duck's head.

Señor Carlos strutted across the yard.

The amiguitos clapped.

"Let's help decorate the other pets," said Liliana.
"Hee-haw," brayed Ana's (Ah-nah) burro.
Ana twirled curls into the burro's mane for the special day.

"Look at my jack rabbit in her pink skirt!" said Elena (ah-LANE-ah),
as she cut holes in a bonnet for the pet's ears.
The rabbit wiggled her long ears.

Tomás (toe-MAHS) washed his cat and wove a garland of flowers for her.

"Prrrrrrrrr," said the cat.

"Come here so I can trim your beard," Manuel (man-WELL) said to his goat.

"Be careful because goats can butt and tip you over," warned Juan.

"And I must watch this goat because he wants to eat my hat!" said Manuel.

When Manuel had finished cutting the beard, Juan painted the goat's hooves yellow.

"Quack, quack, SQUAWK!" said Señor Carlos.
"So much squawking hurts my ears!" said Liliana, shaking her head.
Liliana stroked her duck and gave it some corn.

"Peep, peep, peep," said María's (mah-REE-ah) chicks.
The mother hen clucked and all the chicks ran to her.
"Who can help tie the ribbons around their necks?" asked María.
"Me!" said Elena.
"We'll have a different color for each one," said María.

   "And shall we make a shawl for the hen's neck?" asked Elena.
   María nodded. "Shawls are very important for mothers as they can be used as a coat, or a cradle or a market basket."
   When the shawl was made, the hen and her chicks were set for the blessing.

"My dog can do many tricks," said Gilberto. "He'll be in red velvet pants, so everyone will notice him!"

"R-r-r-r-r-r-r- woof," barked Gilberto's dog.

"I think Señor Carlos likes your dog's pants," said Liliana as the duck walked over to the dog and sat down beside him.

"Señor Carlos is very brave when I am here," said Gilberto, smiling. "He knows my dog will not chase him when I am watching."

"Me, me, me," screeched Nora's (NO-rah) parrot.
"Would you like a bow tie and bells?" asked Nora.
"Yes, yes, yes!" said the parrot in a loud voice.

A tortoise walked slowly toward Señor Carlos.
"Quack, quack, SQUAWK," said the duck, looking down at the
tortoise.
"How can I dress my tortoise for the blessing when he often tucks
his head and legs under his shell?" inquired Roberto (rroh-BER-toe).
"Let's put my toy monkey on his back," suggested Nora.
"That would be fun!" said Roberto.

"That makes uno, dos, tres, cuatro, cinco, seis, siete, ocho, nueve pets," said Liliana. "Where is yours, Juan?"

Juan brought his cow.

"Now we have diez," said Liliana.

"Everyone will look at my cow when the sun, moon and stars are painted on her," said Juan.

The amiguitos helped Juan.

When they were done, Juan added a hat with ribbons and flowers.

Wiggle, wiggle, waddle.
"Quack, quack, SQUAWK!"

"Señor Carlos says the parade should begin!" said Liliana, waving her hand.

The amiguitos had a magnificent parade and soon the children and their pets were at the church across from the plaza.

In front of the church was the padre (PAH-dray).

He counted as he blessed the little friends' pets, "Uno, dos, tres, cuatro, cinco, seis, siete, ocho, nueve, diez."

The last to be blessed was Señor Carlos.

Wiggle, wiggle, waddle.

"Quack, quack, SQUAWK, SQUAWK, SQUAWK ...."

"Where are you going, Señor Carlos?" shouted Liliana, following her duck.

Liliana found Señor Carlos sitting under a bush.

"SQUAWK! SQUAWK! SQUAWK!"

"Why is Señor Carlos making so much noise?" asked the padre, scratching his head.

"Oh, my! Look here!" shouted Liliana.   "SEÑOR CARLOS HAS
LAID AN EGG! SEÑOR CARLOS IS A GIRL!"

Liliana began to laugh.

All the children laughed.

The padre laughed the most of all.

"Señor Carlos was squawking because she was going to lay an
egg!" said Liliana.

"We must tell the village that our amigo Señor Carlos is really
Señorita Carla!" said the padre.

Gilberto pulled on the rope for the church bells.

BONG!   BONG!   BONG!

Everyone came running.

"Bravo, Señorita Carla!" shouted the villagers after they heard that
she had laid an egg. "Let us have a grand fiesta to celebrate!"

The whole village was excited about Señorita Carla's egg. There was a joyous fiesta that lasted until the blue sky was black and studded with stars. Sopaipillas (so-pie-PEE-yas) dipped in honey, enchiladas, and tortillas were brought to the park. The mariachi band played music that started fect dancing, while fireworks splashed merry colors and confetti floated through the air.

Señorita Carla did not go to the fiesta. Instead, she sat faithfully on her egg and did not leave her nest for many days. In time, when her egg was hatched, she proudly led the baby duckling about the village where children live in pink houses, and chili peppers hang by front doors.

Jean Thor Cook is an ardent traveler, finding inspiration for many of her stories in the localities she visits and the people she meets. It was in Columbus, a tiny border town in New Mexico, where she met Judith Donoho Shade and recognized Judy's magical talent for being a children's book illustrator. The story, Los Amiguitos' FIESTA, was written specifically for Judy's engaging " little kids," as she lovingly referred to the characters she drew.

Jean lives in Colorado with her husband Alan, has nine grandchildren, a Bachelor's degree in Elementary Education, and a Master's degree in Adult Education.

Judy Donoho Shade was a loving mother, wife, grandmother and friend to many. Over the years she had also become an accomplished artist in many mediums, from oil paintings and pastels to penciled pictures and sculptures.

Living in the small New Mexico border town of Columbus, Judy's heart led her to the creation of the whimsical kids, " Los Amiguitos." Her soulful characters began as envelope art created with love for her far away mother who was an aging Alzheimer's victim.

Judy passed away in the spring of 1999, far too soon for those who loved her and before she could see this book published. It is with great pride and excitement that we present this book- a gift to our Mom and all of you - from daughters Pam, Kim and Beth. Mom said it best, " Love is the greatest gift! "